ONLY ONE

Marc Harshman

ILLUSTRATED BY Barbara Garrison

COBBLEHILL BOOKS/Dutton · New York

For Cheryl, my only one
M.H.

For Lisa
B.G.

The artwork for this book are collagraphs. The word "collagraph" is made up of "collage" and "graphic." A collagraph plate is made up of pieces of paper and other materials glued down on cardboard which is then inked and printed on an etching press. Once dried, watercolor washes are applied for color.
Materials used for the collagraphs illustrating this book included paper, matboard, sandpaper, paper doilies, paper ribbon, paper stars, masking tape, contact paper, foil, feathers, seed, glitter, sequins, thread, string.

Library of Congress Cataloging-in-Publication Data
Harshman, Marc. Only one / Marc Harshman ; illustrated by Barbara Garrison.
p.   cm.
Summary: At a county fair there are five hundred seeds in one pumpkin, ten cents in one dime, eight horses on one merry-go-round, four wheels on one wagon, and so on.
ISBN 0-525-65116-0   1. Counting—Juvenile literature. [1. Counting. 2. Fairs.
3. Agricultural exhibitions.] I. Garrison, Barbara, ill. II. Title.   QA113.H37
1992   513.2'11—dc20   [E]   92-11349   CIP   AC
Published in the United States by Cobblehill Books, an affiliate of Dutton Children's Books, a division of Penguin Books USA Inc., 375 Hudson Street, New York, New York 10014
Designed by Kathleen Westray   Printed in Hong Kong
First Edition   10   9   8   7   6

There may be a million stars,
But there is only one sky.

There may be 50,000 bees,
But there is only one hive.

There may be 500 seeds,
But there is only one pumpkin.

There may be 100 patches,
But there is only one quilt.

There may be 12 eggs,
But there is only one dozen.

There may be 11 cows,
But there is only one herd.

There may be 10 cents,
But there is only one dime.

There may be 9 players,
But there is only one team.

There may be 8 horses,
But there is only one merry-go-round.

There may be 7 peas,
But there is only one pod.

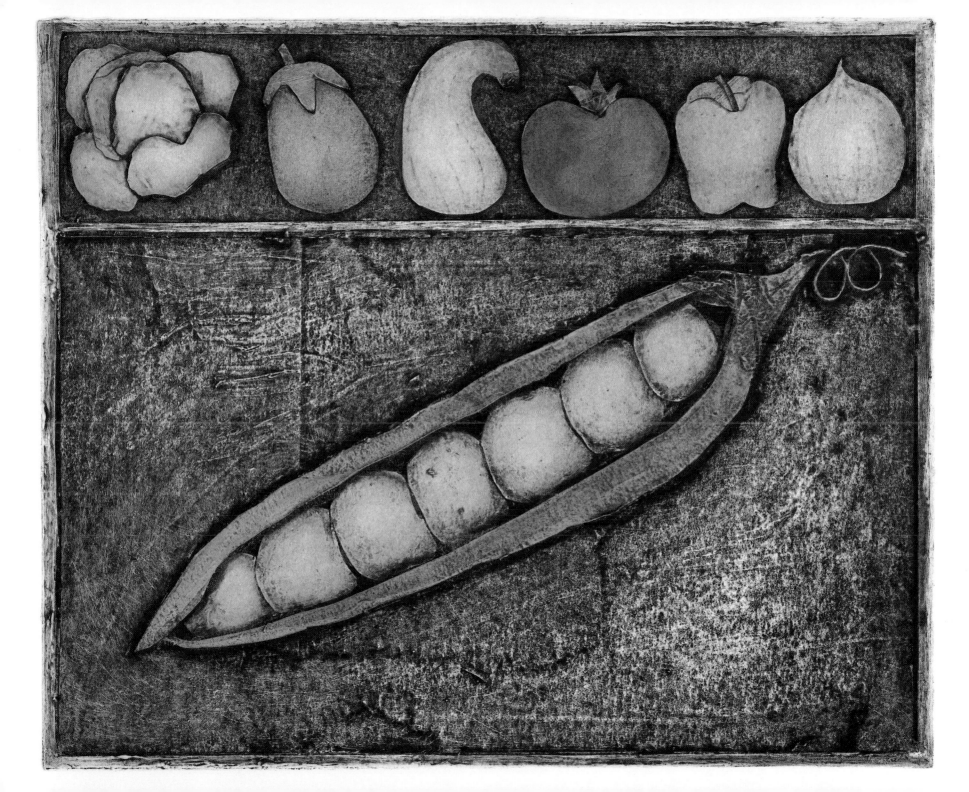

There may be 6 jewels,
But there is only one necklace.

There may be 5 babies,
But there is only one nest.

There may be 4 wheels,
But there is only one wagon.

There may be 3 musicians,
But there is only one trio.

There may be 2 ropes,
But there is only one swing.

But the best thing of all
is that there is only one me
and there is only one you.